Your Name is Sin

Steve Cain

Your Name is Sin

Your Name is Sin is a work of fiction. References to actual persons, places, happenings have been fictionalized. All characters and incidents come from the author's imagination and are not intended as real.

The author maintains full ownership and/or legal rights to publish this work.

Cover design and production by Steve Cain.

More from Steve Cain:

The Great Inevitable, Losantiville Press
Jumpin' Jesus, Hallelujah, Amazon
Thorn, Amazon
The Box of Dreams and Memories, Amazon,
Leave a Message, Amazon,
December Promise, Amazon
The Crow and the Harp, Amazon
Nothing but Sand, Amazon
Dead Birds, Amazon
Bombs and Dragons, Amazon
My Guardian Anger, Amazon
The Silent Shore, Amazon

DEDICATION

This book is dedicated to Frances Partridge, who was a neighbor, a friend, and a second mother and grandmother to me and to my family. We miss you!

CONTENTS

ACKNOWLEDGMENTS

I would like to thank everyone who opens these pages and reads my words and to everyone who follows me on my social media pages. Thank you for your support!

Author's Note

Good day, friend! We're friends, right? The world needs people to be friends. The world needs people to have each other's back, friends to teach each other, to learn from each other, friends to laugh with, friends to cry with, friends to share with. The world needs people to be good to each other.

There's too much division in the world, in our country, in our states, in our communities. Politics does that to us. If they would work for the common good and come to agreement, we could solve many of the problems that we face instead of working on party lines and serving half the country. It's like that in our lives, too. We want what we want, and many times do not take into consideration the needs of others. We could accomplish so much more by compromise.

Getting off my soap box here. I try to be a good person, but it's difficult with so much hate around us. I try to smile because my smile may be the only smile that someone may see that day. I try to be kind because it may be the only kindness someone may find that day. I try to show Jesus in my actions because that may be the only time someone else sees Jesus. No matter your faith, your kindness and love can change the mood and the life of someone else.

As always, I appreciate you reading my words. It means more to me than you know, and I hope you feel inspired by something you read in these pages. Sometimes I'm happy, and my work reflects that. Sometimes I'm sad or lonely, and my writings reflect that. Sometimes I'm angry, and my work reflects that as well. Emotions are what makes us human. Love is what makes us human. Hate is what also makes us human. Having an out let for your emotions is therapy. My writing, my music, my drawings, are my outlets, my therapy. I urge you to find a creative way to express yourself rather than holding your emotions inside. Even if you just write a journal for yourself, getting the emotions out on paper can relieve your mind, keep the demons at bay.

Remember, every interaction you have with people is a

chance to make the world a better place. Smile, wave, nod, say

hello. We can change the world one smile at a time!

The works in this book were written between March and

April 2022.

Steve

Your Name is Sin

Your name is sin.

I breathe you in.

I whisper you.

I taste you,

Bitter and delicious,

Like a dark berry.

You receive,

You deceive.

You bring me down,

You lift me up,

Just to bring me down again,

And again,

And again.

You're not a serpent,

But your tongue is both pleasure and poison.

You have beguiled me,

Defiled me,

Reviled me.

I have been the clay you mold,

The canvas you paint upon,

The paper you have written life on then tossed into the

wastebasket.

You have discarded me,

And I keep turning up with flowers in my hands for you.

I need another fix.

I need another touch.

I need another taste.

I hate you.

I love you.

I hate you.

I have forgotten to not believe the lies.

I want to breathe.

Let me breathe you in,

Again.

<u>Chained</u>

I am chained by the past,

These shackles I've placed upon myself,

Burdened myself with.

I could shrug them off anytime I want,

And I should,

But the fears and the pain gang up on me like love,

Like a warm blanket fresh out of the dryer.

They lie.

I know they lie,

But they feel like friends.

They whisper like angels,

And I know they lie to me,

But it's hard sometimes not to believe the lies,

Hard not to believe that I'm not forgiven,

That I'm not loved,

That I've done all this to myself.

I know what's true,

But I know what's comfortable,

And I know these lies,

And the chains aren't tight.

I can shrug them off whenever I want.

They just feel like a hug,

And I need a hug.

One Knees

I don't need a man

To confess my sins to,

But I know it can help

To talk to someone else.

Today, I'd rather talk to You,

You who hears all,

You who sees all.

You know my heart.

I'm sorry, Lord.

I confess all.

One knees, I cry.

On knees, I pray.

On knees, I bare all.

On knees, I am forgiven.

Lord, I am a sinner.

I fall shirt every day.

I try to lead others,

But I cannot lead myself.

I turn to You.

I surrender to You.

I surrender all.

Only You can wash me clean.

I'm sorry, Lord.

I confess all.

One knees, I cry.

On knees, I pray.

On knees, I bare all.

On knees, I am forgiven.

Thank You, Lord.

Thank You, Lord.

One knees, I cry.

On knees, I pray.

On knees, I bare all.

On knees, I am…

On knees, I cry.

On knees, I pray.

On knees, I bare all.

One knees, I am…

I am forgiven.

I am forgiven.

On knees, I am forgiven

<u>Enough</u>

Enough, enough,

I know who I am.

Enough, enough,

I know.

Enough, enough,

I know where I stand.

Enough,

I know.

Don't look me in the eyes;

You know you beguile me,

And I can't stand it when your eyes shine bright.

You tease me.

You tempt me.

Enough, enough,

I know who I am.

Enough,

I know.

Don't tell me lies.

I won't believe the guise,

But I'll go along with you anyway.

You know I'm fragile

And not too stabile.

Enough, enough,

I know where I stand.

I know.

Enough, okay?

Enough.

It's okay.

I know.

Enemies and Friends

Enemies and friends,

Demons and angels,

Ghouls and fools…

I don't know which are which.

When some lie and others are hypocrites,

The lines get blurred.

White hats with black shirts,

Black hats with white pants,

Who knows who's who?

Maybe they are two halves of the same face,

Two sides of the same coin.

Maybe they're one and the same.

Maybe they are one and the same.

Maybe I am, too.

Maybe I don't know anymore.

I Will Bleed

I will bleed.

I will bleed for you.

It means so little to me,

But it seems to be so much more for you.

I will bleed for you,

But you want the pain that goes with the blood,

The cut,

The jagged wound,

But I'm sorry,

I don't feel that pain anymore.

I just don't feel anymore.

The blood is all you can have.

Too Much Silence

There is too much silence.

(There is silence in silence).

There is too much silence.

(There is silence in silence).

It is too quiet.

No ticking clocks,

No squeaking of broken cart wheels,

No rattling of trays,

No chatter,

No wind breeze,

No bird song,

No ringing in my ears.

My heart is thumping in my chest,

But there is no sound.

I try to shout,

But there is no sound.

I punch the wall,

But there is no sound.

(There is silence in silence).

Am I dead?

I should hear harps or fires,

Something,

Anything,

But there is nothing.

There is no sound of my dry tongue on my dry lips.

(There is silence in silence).

Even my thoughts are quiet.

I shake the door knob,

But there is only silence.

(There is silence in silence).

Where am I?

What did I do?

Can I not speak?

Can I not hear?

No fans,

No white noise,

No Muzak,

No…

Anything.

(There is silence in silence).

I will sit in my corner,

And I will pray,

And I will pray,

And I will listen,

And I will listen,

And maybe I will hear something.

(There is silence in silence).

Something is better than nothing.

(There is silence in silence).

There is nothing but quiet,

Too much silence.

(There is silence in silence).

Too much silence.

Too much.

<u>Let You Down</u>

I am just a man,

And I am not your savior.

I am a sinner.

I am weak because I am flesh.

My thoughts are not pure.

My tongue is too sharp.

If you believe in me,

I will let you down.

I may not always fall,

But I often stumble,

And if you take my hand,

You may stumble, too.

I will show you the map,

I will show you the path,

I will show you the way,

But do not walk in my footsteps.

I will let you down.

I am good.

I try to be good,

But I am not good enough.

I will never be good enough,

But the water and the blood have washed over me,

And I am free.

Don't follow me.

You can walk beside me,

Please,

But don't follow.

I can hold you up,

You can hold me up.

Follow the Light.

Follow the Son.

Man will let you down.

I will let you down.

He will not let you down.

He will never let you down.

American Violence

Guns and power,

Every hour,

Curses and tattoos,

How will that do?

Give me a beer and a shot,

Fireball whiskey, hot.

Drink it down, fools and clowns,

Drinks all around!

Liquid courage,

Raise the flag!

American violence,

The few, the proud.

American violence,

Living loud.

American violence,

Stand your ground.

American violence,

Honor and glory bound.

You want to cross me? Come and try.

Knock you out as these fists fly.

Badass with a hand grenade,

Throwing hands and throwing shade.

Bullet brigade, piledriving soul,

Cross that line and pay the toll.

Not a seal or green beret,

Not today, fool, not today.

Liquid courage,

Raise the flag!

American violence,

The few, the proud.

American violence,

Living loud.

American violence,

Stand your ground.

American violence,

Honor and glory bound.

This is my home,

This is my life,

Picket fence, kids, dogs, and wife.

Shotgun beers, shotgun fears,

No more worries, no more tears.

Made in the U.S.A.

Liquid courage,

Raise the flag.

Liquid courage,

Raise the flag.

Liquid courage,

Raise the flag.

Liquid courage,

Raise the flag!

American violence,

The few, the proud.

American violence,

Living loud.

American violence,

Stand your ground.

American violence,

Honor and glory bound.

American violence,

The few, the proud.

American violence,

Living loud.

American violence,

Stand your ground.

American violence,

Honor and glory,

Honor and glory bound.

Made,

Made in the U.S.A.

<u>Lies and the Fire</u>

I take your lies,

One by one,

And I toss them into the fire.

They burn so hot.

They burn so long.

I toss them on the fire,

And I thank you for your lies.

Gas is high,

Even with my rewards card,

And I haven't the strength to chop wood.

Your lies,

Your lies,

They keep me going.

They'll last all winter,

Maybe longer.

I have them stored up where they'll stay dry,

Waiting,

Ready to burn.

Ready.

Ready to burn.

They burn so hot.

The Flower

It could lie dormant no longer.

It yawned,

It stretched,

And when it stretched,

The moist dirt above its head yielded,

Opening slowly like a cervix.

A golden sun burst through as the earth gave birth to the flower.

The yellow face turned upwards to greet the warmth of the sun for

the first time,

Its leaves reaching out to touch the breeze.

Life! Sweet life!

It took in the sounds of the birds in the trees singing their lullabies.

Tired,

So tired,

The flower bowed its head after all its effort.

The morning dew settled on the petals,

And a cautious bee sampled its nectar.

Life! Sweet life!

Such a sensory overload!

The flower rested as the sun smiled down from the heavens.

There will be more,

More to see,

To hear,

To feel,

But for now, rest.

Rest.

There will be time for life.

Life!

Sweet, sweet life!

Hide, Seek, Sink

Sink down,

Under the water.

Sink down,

Under the water.

Carbon dioxide bubbles.

I pinch my nose.

They won't find me.

They can't find me here.

Hide and seek.

They'll never look for me here.

They'll stop looking and go home.

They'll go home and never find me.

Carbon dioxide bubbles.

Pinch my nose.

Hold my breath.

Soon now.

Bricks,

Ropes.

They'll never find me.

I bet they won't even look.

<u>Schrodinger's Casket</u>

Is he still in there,

Or is he gone?

Is he alive,

Or is he done?

Should we knock?

Should we yell?

Is he there,

Or in Heaven, Hell?

Schrodinger's casket.

Schrodinger's casket.

Should we bury it,

Put it into the ground?

What if we open it,

And he's not found?

Hey, Bob, can you hear me?

Isn't this fun?

Let's open it

On 3, 2, 1.

Schrodinger's casket.

Schrodinger's casket.

Wait, what are we doing?

We have to go.

Bob's been in there

Four hours or so.

If he didn't get out,

And we shut him in,

He's gotta be dead, right?

Killing's a sin!

Schrodinger's casket.

Schrodinger's casket.

Shhh, just walk away.

We were never here.

I'll wipe it down,

Wipe the fingerprints clear.

Bob knew the risks.

He didn't have to get in.

We don't know if he's out,

Or if he's still in.

Schrodinger's casket.

Schrodinger's casket.

Did you hear a knock?

Bob?

I think we should just go.

<u>Might Start a War</u>

Who can I offend today?

Maybe I'll get offended.

Maybe a slap,

Maybe a punch,

Just might start a war.

Maybe a word,

Maybe a gesture,

Maybe I just don't care.

Maybe it's all for fun.

Just might start a war.

I don't care for your bombs or planes.

I don't care how you sound or look.

It has nothing to do with me at all.

It's all me, it's all mine.

Just might start a war.

It's not irony.

It's not hatred.

It's not gluttony.

It's not blasphemy.

Just might start a war.

I'm tired of movies.

I'm tired of books.

I'm tired of music.

I'm tired of talk.

Just might start a war.

I'm not about conquest.

I'm not about power.

I'm not about borders.

I'm not about control.

Just might start a war.

I see you coming down the street.

I don't even care who you are.

I'll get your whole family, too.

I don't care what you say or do.

I just might start a war.

Let's have some fun.

Let's have a ball.

Let's destroy,

Let's destroy it all.

Just might start a war.

Are you ready?

Are you scared?

Gonna start a war.

Love to start a war.

Just might start a war.

The Rock That Rolled

Jesus, son of God,

Overcame the world.

Scorned, mocked, beaten,

He denied the underworld.

Scourged and bloodied,

Nail to a tree.

Three days later,

The tomb was empty.

You and I,

He paid for our crimes.

The rock that rolled

Couldn't hold His soul.

Resurrected, He is risen

Out of death's hold.

It is finished, Jesus said,

And He gave up the ghost.

He was pulled down from

That old wooden post.

Covered and shrouded,

Placed in a grave.

On Easter, no body

Was found in that cave.

You and I,

He paid for our crimes.

The rock that rolled

Couldn't hold His soul.

Resurrected, He is risen

Out of death's hold.

You and I,

He paid for our crimes.

The rock that rolled

Couldn't hold His soul.

Resurrected, He is risen

Out of death's hold.

The rock that rolled

Couldn't hold His soul.

Resurrected, He is risen,

Resurrected, He is risen,

Resurrected, He is risen!

War Drums

Hear the beat

In the city streets.

There's a battle looming

In the raging heat.

Demons march,

Angels in the air.

Swords of fire,

Armor shining everywhere.

War drums,

Percussion pounding for the lord.

Ward drums,

Feel it down into your core.

War drums,

Beating out a victory.

War drums,

Revelation history.

Trumpets blaring,

Heaven's soldiers on the attack.

Enemy,

Hellish warriors get pushed back.

See the keys,

Unlock the gates to the abyss.

Hear the demons

Cry and curse and gnash and hiss.

War drums,

Percussion pounding for the lord.

Ward drums,

Feel it down into your core.

War drums,

Beating out a victory.

War drums,

Revelation history.

See them kneel,

Fallen angels beaten down.

See Him rise,

Jesus, King of Kings is crowned.

War drums,

Percussion pounding for the lord.

Ward drums,

Feel it down into your core.

War drums,

Beating out a victory.

War drums,

Revelation history.

Beating out a history,

Revelation history.

Jesus, King of Kings is crowned.

<u>Fragile Things</u>

Fragile things,

Like butterfly wings,

And love,

Stained glass,

And light bulbs,

And good intents.

Friendships,

Vows,

Ceramic clowns,

Skin and eyes,

A thin disguise.

Such fragile things,

Like a lover sings

Of his heart,

And his love departs.

Pages in books,

And a babbling brook

Rippled by a stone,

Finger bones,

Chicken eggs,

And coffee dregs.

The things she said,

Hanging over my head,

Fragile in her words,

Like ladybirds.

Fragile, to be held close,

To be loved more than most

And locked away

To keep the wolves at bay.

Yes, lock it away

Where it can't be betrayed (or betray),

For it (she) is fragile

And not so agile,

And still it beats,

So, we'll keep it discreet,

Shall we?

Indeed?

My secret is yours;

That's what all this is for.

All these fragile things,

Like my guitar strings,

Strumming out a love song

That didn't belong.

Such fragile, fragile things,

Like the reign of kings,

And the chill that winter brings.

So fragile, like the candlelight,

And how it penetrates the night.

So fragile, and I know

Which way the winds blow,

And it will change.

It will always change,

As the winds are fragile, too,

And we are as well, I and you,

Such fragile things.

<u>Love Over Mind</u>

She can see,

But she doesn't know it's me,

But still she smiles,

And love is all she knows.

What's on her mind?

The past and time have merged.

Confusion,

But love is all she knows.

She don't know.

She don't know.

She don't know,

But she doesn't have to know,

Doesn't have to know to love,

Because love over mind.

Love is stronger.

I see the lines

On her face and on her hands.

She doesn't talk,

But her smile says everything.

It's so unfair

When your memories go away,

But still she shows

That love is better.

She don't know.

She don't know.

She don't know,

But she doesn't have to know,

Doesn't have to know to love,

Because love over mind.

Love is stronger.

She can see,

But she doesn't know it's me,

But still she smiles,

And love is all she knows.

And still she shows

That love is better.

Love is better.

She don't know.

She don't know.

She don't know,

But she doesn't have to know,

Doesn't have to know to love,

Because love over mind.

Love is stronger.

Because love over mind.

Love is stronger.

Love is stronger.

Villain

You blame me,

O take it.

I'm not mad.

Maybe once,

But not now.

It's easier for you to hate me,

To place the blame on me,

Than it is to face it yourself.

It's okay;

You're not strong like me.

You need people to hear you,

To see you,

To love you,

To pity you.

I am strong and content in my isolation

Because my isolation is sunshine,

Flowers,

Pine needle,

Rain,

Peace.

It's okay.

You have my blessing,

But if you choose me to be the villain,

Remember there's a part to play,

And,

Thespian that I may be,

I must play that part.

You make me the villain,

The villain I shall be,

And you will have to live with everything that comes from that.

Everything.

I will play the role you cast me in,

And you can't call, "Cut!"

You can't call, "Scene!"

You can't clear the set.

I will always stay in character.

Blacktop Hurricane

Drive! Drive!

Gonna try to break the speed of sound.

Move! Move!

Gone burn the rubber to the ground.

Lights! Lights!

Streetlights, headlights all a blur.

Night! Night!

As I push the pedal to the floor.

Sound and fury,

Vision getting blurry.

Wind in my hair.

Where I'm going, I don't care.

Driving like a blacktop hurricane.

Driving like a blacktop hurricane.

High! High!

I feel the rush of adrenaline.

Time! Time!

Nowhere to go, got a full tank of gasoline.

Speed! Speed!

Going a hundred in a sixty-five.

Loud! Loud!

Hard rocking music got me feeling alive.

Sound and fury,

Vision getting blurry.

Wind in my hair.

Where I'm going, I don't care.

Driving like a blacktop hurricane.

Driving like a blacktop hurricane.

Speed! Speed!

Going a hundred in a sixty-five.

Loud! Loud!

Sirens blaring, but they're never gonna take me alive.

Sound and fury,

Vision getting blurry.

Wind in my hair.

Where I'm going, I don't care. (I don't care)

Driving like a blacktop hurricane.

Driving like a blacktop hurricane.

Sound and fury,

Vision getting blurry.

Wind in my hair.

Where I'm going, I don't care. (I don't care)

Driving like a blacktop hurricane.

Driving like a blacktop hurricane.

Driving like a blacktop hurricane.

Driving like a blacktop,

A blacktop hurricane!

What to Do

Don't touch my leg,

It's ticklish.

What about your lips?

Oh, I don't kiss.

Well, what do you do?

I tell you what to do,

That's what I do.

How about a hug?

No, you say with a shrug.

Holding hands?

No, that's not the plan.

Well, what do you do?

I tell you what to do,

That's what I do.

Fold the clothes,

Wash the dishes,

Go get milk.

That's what I do because that's what you told me I could do.

Cut the grass,

Take out the dogs,

Go get bread.

That's what I do because that's what you tell me I can do.

Can we get into bed?

There's an ache in my head.

Well, what can we do?

We can sleep,

And you can do what I tell you to do,

Like I always do.

That's what you can do.

That's all you can do.

<u>Sinsanity</u>

You do the same things over and over,

A few drinks every night,

A few tokes to make it tight,

But the pain doesn't go away.

Drown yourself in lust and pills,

A new danger, a few cheap thrills.

You take a shower to wash it off,

But it just won't wash away.

Only His blood,

Only His blood can cleanse.

Sinsanity,

Hiding away in your sin.

Sinsanity,

A war you'll never win.

Sinsanity,

You know you're living a lie.

Sinsanity,

It's time to say goodbye.

Family and friends try to help you,

But you have to want it for yourself.

No one can do it for you.

Call on Jesus for His help.

He'll guide you through the pain,

Help you through your suffering.

He will forgive all your sins.

He already knows everything

Only His blood,

Only His blood can cleanse.

Sinsanity,

Hiding away in your sin.

Sinsanity,

A war you'll never win.

Sinsanity,

You know you're living a lie.

Sinsanity,

It's time to say goodbye.

Only His blood,

Only His blood can cleanse.

Sinsanity,

Hiding away in your sin.

Sinsanity,

A war you'll never win.

Sinsanity,

You know you're living a lie.

Sinsanity,

It's time to say goodbye.

Sinsanity,

Hiding away in your sin.

Sinsanity,

A war you'll never win.

Sinsanity,

You know you're living a lie.

Sinsanity,

It's time to say goodbye to your old life.

It's time to say goodbye.

Say goodbye.

Fixated

My eyes are fixated,

But you seem so pixilated,

So blurry,

So damned blurry,

I can't get a line on your features.

I'm a creature,

Loathsome,

Ugly,

But I know you're beautiful,

You have to be beautiful.

You have to be beautiful

Because the monster always gets the beautiful girl in the movies.

She always falls in love with the creature.

Have another drink;

I'm buying.

Maybe that'll help.

Doesn't work for me;

I can't see crap anyway,

But I know you're beautiful.

You have that beautiful smell.

Yes, you smell beautiful.

I don't know what I smell like,

But it's probably earthy.

Have another drink;

I'm buying.

Do you love me yet?

I wish I could see you clearly.

Damn.

Damn my eyes.

You have to be beautiful, though.

Come on and kiss the frog.

Do you love me yet?

I could be a prince.

Do you love me yet?

<u>Your Name</u>

I wake saying your name.

I sleep saying your name.

I dream saying your name.

I find myself at work,

Typing your name on my computer,

Over and over.

I call coworkers,

Friends,

By your name.

I see it in print:

In books,

In magazines,

In newspapers.

I hear it in songs,

In movies,

On tv shows.

Everywhere I've looked,

Painted in graffiti on bridges and railcars,

On the sides of buildings.

Your name.

You haunt me,

And I don't why.

I don't know why.

You are the fly buzzing around my head.

You are the ringing in my ears.

You are the wrecking ball demolishing the building I sleep in.

You are the rooster that wakes me in the morning

And the lullaby that sings me to sleep at night.

Your name.

You are confusion,

Conundrum,

Mystery,

Enigma,

Chaos.

You are the labyrinth and the minotaur.

You are the cave and the bat.

You are the disease and the cure,

The drink,

The pill,

The hangover,

The calm,

The storm,

The rainbow.

You are the promise,

The lie.

You are the scream,

The echo,

The silence.

You are the blessed and the damned,

And so am I.

You are the blood,

And I am the wine,

And we have drunk of each other,

Been drunk on each other.

We are both warden and prisoner.

You are the key and the cell,

And I am never free.

I call your name,

And you hear me,

But you come when it suits you.

I looked up at the sun today,

And all I saw in the blur was your name,

Burnt into my retina.

You are tattooed on my skin,

And you clog my arteries.

Your name.

You will be the death of me,

Just as you've been the life.

Your name is life and death,

And either way,

I am never free.

In Heaven they will sing your name.

In Hell they will scream it.

Either way,

I will never be free.

Broken Circle

Life is like a roulette wheel:

Fast, a blur, I don't know what's real.

Friends in high school, college, work,

Girls you loved now think you're a jerk.

Social media expands your scene,

Three thousand friends you've never seen.

Who can you talk to, who can you trust?

So many quick to leave you in the dust.

Broken circle,

One goes out, one goes in,

Spinning round and round again.

Friends and lovers come and go.

Broken circle,

Round and round and round it goes,

And where it stops, no one knows.

But the world keeps spinning.

The world keeps spinning.

Knife in the back, a smile to your face.

These friends leave without a trace.

You don't need them, and that's the truth.

Keep your circle to a chosen few.

The smaller the circle, the stronger the bond.

They're the ones who'll go beyond

Your expectations, keep them close.

Family are the ones you chose

Broken circle,

One goes out, one goes in,

Spinning round and round again.

Friends and lovers come and go.

Broken circle,

Round and round and round it goes,

And where it stops, no one knows.

But the world keeps spinning.

The world keeps spinning.

Broken circle,

One goes out, one goes in,

Spinning round and round again.

Friends and lovers come and go.

Broken circle,

Round and round and round it goes,

And where it stops, no one knows.

But the world keeps spinning.

The world keeps spinning.

Press the Button

Pain, pain, pain!

Drip, drip, drip.

More pain, more pain.

Press the button,

Drip, drip, drip.

Feel the heat coursing through the veins.

Drip, drip, drip.

Brown Heaven.

Feel nothing,

For a while.

I see why they call it God's Drug.

Feel like I'm flying,

Floating,

Slowly,

Clouds whipping by my face.

I'm at peace.

Relief.

I feel my heartbeat slow.

Pain, pain, pain!

Press the button,

Quick!

Drip, drip, drip.

I feel nothing,

Nothing but tired.

I don't have a care.

Drip, drip, drip.

Press the button.

Drip, drip, drip.

I don't care.

Press the button.

Drip, drip, drip.

I don't care.

Press the button.

Drip, drip, drip.

I don't...

Trail of Teardrops

I can't believe it ended this way.

You couldn't even tell me why.

It took a while before I could even walk away,

Standing in a puddle from my eyes.

If you come back, you'll find me gone.

There isn't any reason to stay.

You made it clear that I didn't belong,

And now the skies are dark and gray.

If you want to find me,

If you want to find me,

If you want to find me,

Just follow my trail of teardrops.

My feet are wet and leaving tracks.

It doesn't even matter anymore.

My heart has had me tripping over cracks,

Like we've done so many times before.

You were growing, leaning towards the sun.

I was withered, rooted in my place.

It was over before it had begun.

I'd water you with teardrops from my face,

But if you want to find me,

If you want to find me,

If you want to find me,

Just follow my trail of teardrops.

Want to walk, want to run,

Want to hide out from the sun.

Maybe I'm better off with someone,

Someone who doesn't make me feel this way.

If you want to find me,

If you want to find me,

If you want to find me,

Just follow…

If you want to find me,

If you want to find me,

If you want to find me,

Just follow,

Just follow,

Just follow my trail of teardrops.

I'm Not There

You spat,

And you spewed,

And you cursed,

And the droplets fell down on me like acid rain

It burned,

And it burned,

And I allowed it.

I allowed your words

And your palms,

And you fists,

And your kicks,

And the soles of your feet walking over me,

Spikes digging into my back,

And the blood flowed,

And you never cared,

And you never cared.

I took and I took,

And I took more.

Now you're cursing and spewing and spitting,

And you're looking,

And you're searching,

And you can't find me to slap,

To punch,

To kick,

To walk upon.

You can't find me because I'm not there.

I'm not there,

And you'll have to curse me while you spit on someone else.

I'm through with that.

I'm not there,

And I'll never be there again.

<u>Where's Your Faith?</u>

There are three doors before you.

One will allow you to wake from this dream.

One will open to gate to Heaven.

One will open the doorway to Hell.

Which one will you choose?

Which One will you choose?

There are three doors before you.

One is blue like the sky.

One is the color of polished gold.

One is as black as night.

Which one will you choose?

Which One will you choose?

You have a choice to make.

Where's your faith?

The choice is yours.

Where's your faith?

There are three doors before you.

What do you believe?

Looks can be deceiving,

But so is the heart.

Which one will you choose?

Which One will you choose?

There are three doors before you.

Make sure to pray.

Open your mind and your heart

And reach for a knob.

Which one will you choose?

Which One will you choose?

You have a choice to make.

Where's your faith?

The choice is yours.

Where's your faith?

The lady or the tiger?

Hell or paradise?

Maybe you'll just wake up,

But one day you'll have to choose.

Which one will you choose?

Which One will you choose?

I see you close your eyes.

I see your lips move.

I see the sweat on your forehead.

You reach for a door.

Which did you choose?

Which One did you choose?

You have a choice.

Where's your faith?

The choice is yours.

Where's your faith?

There are three doors before you.

Which do you choose?

Where's your faith?

Chupa Dupa

You think I'm a dog?

No way, muchacho.

I'm a heteropalindrome.

That means I'm a god.

Where do I live?

Wherever I want.

From Maine to 'Zona,

Puerto Rico to 'Zuela.

Beware my bite.

Beware my claws.

Super-duper beast, baby.

You're gonna get it all.

I'm a Chupacabra,

Chupa Dupa.

Chupacabra,

Chupa Dupa.

Chupacabra,

Chupa Dupa.

I'm a Chupacabra,

Chupa Dupa.

They call me goat sucker.

I'll take your life.

Bite your hand,

Lick your wife.

I'm not a dingo,

But I'll steal your babe.

Triangle bite,

Get outta my way.

Beware my bite.

Beware my claws.

Super-duper beast, baby.

You're gonna get it all.

I'm a Chupacabra,

Chupa Dupa.

Chupacabra,

Chupa Dupa.

Chupacabra,

Chupa Dupa.

I'm a Chupacabra,

Chupa Dupa.

See my big, long…tail

And my lizard tongue.

Gonna eat ya, baby,

Come and get ya some.

Beware my bite.

Beware my claws.

Super-duper beast, baby.

You're gonna get it all.

I'm a Chupacabra,

Chupa Dupa.

Chupacabra,

Chupa Dupa.

Chupacabra,

Chupa Dupa.

I'm a Chupacabra,

Chupa Dupa.

Come and get ya some.

Vibrations

(In memory of Tim Hagan)

The line ran across the screen,

And there was nothing to do but turn away.

There were no blips,

No beeps,

Just silence.

The lights flickered once,

Twice.

There was a distinct hum like electricity,

And the room pulsed.

I could feel vibrations in the floor,

The walls,

The air,

Vibrations of my friend,

The Harvard graduate,

The chemist,

The quantum physicist,

The cyclist,

The climber,

The beer drink at First and 10,

My friend.

Even in the end,

Showing how smart he was,

Showing that life doesn't end.

We are but energy inside a shell,

And that energy gets released into the world,

Int the void,

Vibrating on a different plane of existence we can't always see.

Sometimes we are given a glimpse,

And we call them ghosts,

Or angels.

My friend is an angel.

I feel his vibes.

I feel his vibrations.

He has transcended.

<u>Let the Wicked Fall</u>

I call to You, Lord, come quickly.

Hear me when I call upon You.

May my prayer be set here before You.

May the lifting of my hands be sacrifice.

Set a guard over my mouth to watch my lips, Lord.

Don't let my heart be drawn towards evil.

Steer me away from all the wicked doers.

Keep me away from all their delicacies.

My eyes are fixed on You, Lord.

My eyes are fixed on You, Lord.

In You I take refuge.

I fix my eyes on You.

Let the wicked fall into their own nets.

We'll escape the trap they've tried to set.

We've tried to make them see, they choose to forget,

So, let the wicked fall,

Let the wicked fall,

Let the wicked fall into their own nets.

Let a righteous man strike me, that is kindness.

Let him rebuke me, let the oil anoint.

I know my hy head will not refuse the blessing.

My prayers against the wicked stand.

Rulers of the wicked shall be cast down.

And they will know my words were spoken well.

They'll say, "as one plows and breaks up the earth,

So our bones have been scattered at the grave."

My eyes are fixed on You, Lord.

My eyes are fixed on You, Lord.

In You I take refuge.

I fix my eyes on You.

Let the wicked fall into their own nets.

We'll escape the trap they've tried to set.

We've tried to make them see, they choose to forget,

So, let the wicked fall,

Let the wicked fall,

Let the wicked fall into their own nets.

My eyes are fixed on You, Lord.

My eyes are fixed on You, Lord.

In You I take refuge.

I fix my eyes on You.

Let the wicked fall into their own nets.

We'll escape the trap they've tried to set.

We've tried to make them see, they choose to forget,

So, let the wicked fall,

Let the wicked fall,

Let the wicked fall,

Let the wicked fall,

Let the wicked fall.

<u>Weighing Me Down</u>

It hurts to breathe.

Between the smoke and deceit,

They're killing me,

But I won't die yet.

No, I won't die yet.

That's what you want,

But I won't die yet.

No, not yet.

The haze hangs thick,

And the air is cold.

Burdened by hate,

I'm feeling gray and old.

Gray and old,

So gray and old,

But I won't die yet.

No, I won't die yet.

Many things left undone.

Many things left unsaid.

My skin,

These bones,

Are weighing me down,

Weighing me down.

My skin,

These bones,

Just weighing me down,

Down, down.

The cough is bad.

There's blood in my spit.

What I know is

That it's come to this,

But I won't die yet.

That's what you want,

But I won't die yet.

Joints are creaking,

I'm ready to snap,

And I know

That I could really use a nap,

But there's too much to do,

So much to do,

And I won't die yet.

No, I won't die yet.

Many things left undone.

Many things left unsaid.

My skin,

These bones,

Are weighing me down,

Weighing me down.

My skin,

These bones,

Just weighing me down,

Down, down.

I won't die yet.

No, I won't die yet.

I know that's what you want,

So, I won't die yet.

Just to spite you,

I won't die yet.

That's what you want,

But I won't die yet.

Many things to do.

Many things to spite you.

My skin,

These bones,

Are weighing me down,

Weighing me down.

My skin,

These bones,

Just weighing me down,

Down, down.

Down, down, down.

Down, down, down.

Pedestal

I put you on a pedestal.

That was my fault.

I loved you.

I admired you.

I thought you were perfect.

I put you on a pedestal

And allowed you to look down on me.

From there,

I could see all the flaws,

The chinks in the armor,

The cracks in the marble.

I out you there and made you more than you are,

An ideal,

An idea.

I was wrong.

I ahd to bring you back down to be able to love you again.

I had to knock you down to admire you again.

You're not perfect.

I'm not perfect.

I love your flaws.

I need you beside me,

Not high above me,

Not on some pedestal.

Black Widow

Red on black,

Like a heart attack.

I feel the venom

Coursing through my veins.

Heartless, cold,

All alone,

Rotting my soul,

She's rotting my brain.

Caught in her snare.

How was I so unaware?

Black widow,

I never saw you coming.

Black widow,

I should've been running.

Black widow,

You're evil and divine.

Black widow,

I'm running out of time.

Head dizzy,

You've been busy.

Others flies in your web,

You're insatiable,

Legs numb,

How was I so dumb?

Fiber's too strong,

Your web's unbreakable.

Caught in her snare.

How was I so unaware?

Black widow,

I never saw you coming.

Black widow,

I should've been running.

Black widow,

You're evil and divine.

Black widow,

I'm running out of time.

Caught in her snare.

How was I so unaware?

Black widow,

I never saw you coming.

Black widow,

I should've been running.

Black widow,

You're evil and divine.

Black widow,

I'm running out of time.

Black widow,

I'm running out of t-i-i-i-ime.

I'm running out of time.

Your New Reality

A thousand eyes that never see,

Caught up in a dream,

A virtual reality

Where nothing is what it seems.

See the parade,

The pretty colors on display,

Vibrant hues in every shade

Beckoning of us to play, all day.

There's something in the peripheral

That just isn't quite visual.

Something old, something residual?

We're catered to the individual.

Do you want sex, vacation, power?

Food, drink, violence every hour?

Sandy beaches, fields with flowers?

Mountain castle with a shiny tower?

You can have it, look and see.

Just don't look over here at me.

You can be what you wanted to be.

Behind these glasses, you are free.

Do you want love and peace and joy?

A garage full of motorized toys?

A spouse and a girl and a boy?

It's all real for you, not a decoy.

You can have it all, put on the shades.

Open a world that we have made.

Don't worry if you think you're played.

Instead of this world of hate and pain, would you trade?

Put them on, accept our gift.

Watch as the scenes and colors shift.

It's a culture shift, a mind shift.

Let's heal this rift.

You know what you want to do.

Take a trip to Mars or to the moon.

You'll never have to worry, you're immune.

Just watch, dear. I'll check on you soon.

You and all the others,

All your new sisters and brothers.

We are your father and your mother.

It's time to harvest another.

Send her in.

Let us begin.

Divide and Survive

This is your last warning;

You won't be told again.

Disperse, move along.

Nothing to see here.

There's no reason

To be on streets.

No need to gather.

No need to meet.

We will tell you what you need to know.

We will show you what you need to see.

Divide and survive

If you want to live.

United you will fall.

Divide and survive.

Forget your friends,

Forget your family.

We are all

That you now need.

Get to your homes,

Turn on your screens.

Throw down your weapons,

You have no need.

We will tell you what you need to know.

We will show you what you need to see.

Divide and survive

If you want to live.

United you will fall.

Divide and survive.

You have no choice;

You can't resist.

We are your parents.

We are your gods.

Go home to your screens,

Go home to your altars.

Kneel down and pray.

We will deliver you.

We will tell you what you need to know.

We will show you what you need to see.

Divide and survive

If you want to live.

United you will fall.

Divide and survive.

United you will fall.

United you will fall.

United you will fall.

Divide and survive.

<u>With My Last Breaths</u>

With my last breaths,

I sing for you,

For us,

For our love.

I breathe you in and sing you out.

With my last breaths,

I give thanks,

For you being sent to me,

For our life,

For our love.

With my last breaths,

I pray,

For you,

For our family,

For peace and comfort,

For our love.

With my last breaths,

I breathe you in and sing you out.

I sing for you,

For us,

For our love.

I sing for you.

<u>Decompose</u>

I like my women after they've died.

It's always better on the other side.

There's nothing like their frigid flesh.

That's the girl that I love best.

No remorse.

I love a corpse.

No remorse.

I love a corpse.

Decompose?

Well, I propose.

It's a marriage made in Hell.

Decompose?

Yes, I propose.

Do I hear wedding bells?

I love to find them just before

They are taken to the morgue.

Call her Alice, call her Jane.

They always love me for my brain.

No remorse.

I love a corpse.

No remorse.

I love a corpse.

Decompose?

Well, I propose.

It's a marriage made in Hell.

Decompose?

Yes, I propose.

Do I hear wedding bells?

There's nothing like that frigid flesh.

That's the girl that I love best.

No remorse.

I love a corpse.

No remorse.

I love a corpse.

Decompose?

Well, I propose.

It's a marriage made in Hell.

Decompose?

Yes, I propose.

Do I hear wedding bells?

Do I hear wedding bells?

Yes, I hear wedding bells.

Pain and Vengeance

You think you can cut me

And just walk away?

You think you can gut me

And leave me to die today?

I will shove my guts back in.

I will sew myself shut.

I will wipe the blood from my hands,

And I will stand up (Stand up).

And when I do…

And when I do…

Pain and vengeance,

My fury will rain.

Pain and vengeance,

Trauma to the brain.

Pain and vengeance,

You'll look in my eyes.

Pain and vengeance,

The last thing you see when you die.

My face is swollen.

My eyes have turned black,

But I'm more than the fallen.

Guess what? I'm back!

You will see me coming,

But there's no use running.

You will see me coming,

And I'm taking my time (Taking my time).

And when I do…

And when I do…

Pain and vengeance,

My fury will rain.

Pain and vengeance,

Trauma to the brain.

Pain and vengeance,

You'll look in my eyes.

Pain and vengeance,

The last thing you see when you die.

You will see me coming,

But there's no use running.

You will see me coming,

And I'm taking my time (Taking my time).

And when I do…

And when I do…

Pain and vengeance,

My fury will rain.

Pain and vengeance,

Trauma to the brain.

Pain and vengeance,

You'll look in my eyes.

Pain and vengeance,

The last thing you see when you die.

And when I do…

And when I do…

Pain and vengeance,

My fury will rain.

Pain and vengeance,

Trauma to the brain.

Pain and vengeance,

You'll look in my eyes.

Pain and vengeance,

The last thing you see when you die.

Look into my eyes!

<u>Dream Specter</u>

You haunt me in my dreams.

Why do you haunt me?

What do you want?

Faceless,

Androgynous,

Are you friend or foe?

You never say or do anything;

You're just…

There.

When I wake,

I sometimes see you out of the corner of my eye,

Just for an instant.

I no longer know what's real;

The lines blur between the conscious and the subconscious.

It always seems to be twilight.

Why, specter?

Why me?

Are you angel or demon?

Are you just watching,

Recording?

Must be pretty boring watching me.

Are you sending a warning?

Why do you just stand there?

What do you want?

Will you just say something?

Anything?

Six months now,

And nothing!

Wait,

Where are you going?

Don't leave!

Come back!

Tell me what you want.

I need to know.

Don't leave.

I didn't mean to run you away.

I need to know,

Please.

What did you want with me?

<u>We Are at War</u>

We are at war.

We are at war.

We are at war.

We are at war.

Turn on your televisions.

Log into your social media.

All you see are lies and division.

You hear what they wanna feed ya.

Algorithms and red herrings,

False flags and hired protests.

It doesn't matter what platform you choose;

They're putting you to the test.

Divide and conquer,

That's their plan.

Divide and conquer,

United we stand.

We are at war.

We are at war.

We are at war.

We are at war.

Friends and neighbors are the enemy.

That's what they tell you from the television screen.

We are all racists; we are all sexists.

They drive a wedge between you and me.

Viral video, they choose the shot.

Only show a clip of what they want

So you can't see the entire truth.

We are at war, a coup d'tat.

Divide and conquer,

That's their plan.

Divide and conquer,

United we stand.

We are at war.

We are at war.

We are at war.

We are at war.

The eye is the lamp of the body (Open your eyes).

He who has an ear, let him hear (Open your ears).

The eye is the lamp of the body (Open your eyes).

He who has an ear, let him hear (Open your ears).

We are at war (War).

We are at war (War).

We are at war (War).

We are at war (War).

We are at war (War).

We are at war (War).

We are at war (War).

We are at war (War).

War!

War!

War!

War!

War!

<u>Tinkering</u>

We are not alone.

We are dreams and nightmares cloned.

I am you,

And you are I,

Angel wings and devil eyes.

Torn up,

Mixed up,

Puzzle pieces that don't quite fit,

Jammed together and glued in place anyway.

We make a pretty picture in an ugly frame.

Aren't you glad you came?

You are like "Sunflowers."

I am like "The Scream."

Together,

We are more like "American Gothic,"

But don't let them know we know.

They don't like it when we know things.

We are made and remade and rearranged.

They're never completely pleased.

I see their paints,

Their clays,

Their charcoals.

I see their belts,

Their pulleys,

Their gears,

Their switches,

Their valves,

And their shafts with their keyways.

I see their hammers,

Their drills,

Their screwdrivers,

Their ratchets.

They're busy,

Always busy,

Tweaking this,

Turning that,

Adjusting,

Measuring,

Cutting,

Adding,

Removing,

Tinkering.

They'll never get it right.

They'll never get us right.

They want perfection.

We were never meant to be perfect.

Hell,

We were never meant to be.

<u>I Died Today</u>

Where have you been?

Where are you going?

I don't know what to sy.

I don't know what to do.

It's a crazy world.

Sometimes the clouds are gray,

Then the skies erupt into sunshine.

That's what happened today.

From across the room,

Across the gallery,

You smiled.

I died today.

You took my breath away,

I couldn't breathe.

I saw you,

And my heart stopped.

Your lips revived me.

I died today,

And now I live again.

There was a glass of wine,

And a look.

No words had to be said.

The eyes said it all.

A touch of your hand,

How your hair fell across your face.

A twinkle there,

In the corner of your eye.

From across the room,

Across the gallery,

You smiled.

I died today.

You took my breath away,

I couldn't breathe.

I saw you,

And my heart stopped.

Your lips revived me.

I died today,

And now I live again.

All the Van Goghs,

The Picassos,

The Renoirs,

They are nothing compared to you.

From across the room,

Across the gallery,

You smiled.

I died today.

You took my breath away,

I couldn't breathe.

I saw you,

And my heart stopped.

Your lips revived me.

I died today,

And now I live again.

I died today,

And now I live again.

<u>The Bleeding Years</u>

I have loved from near and far.

I have haunted churches and bars,

Searching for something,

Something…

I know that God is love,

And is all the I need from above,

But I keep searching for something,

Something…

My support system is low,

Nobody cares.

What I can do is read and write,

Love and pray every day.

These are the bleeding years.

These are the bleeding years.

I see so many others,

Large families, circles of friends,

And I want that, too.

I want that.

I give my support and love

To those who won't reciprocate,

And like a fool, I keep doing,

I keep doing.

That's my insanity,

To think that today will be different,

But it never is.

It never is.

These are the bleeding years.

These are the bleeding years.

All I want is for people to hear me,

To value me,

But all they say is cheer up, buck up, you're wrong.

I'm always wrong.

Turn to God, get some help,

Please don't hurt yourself.

I know God, and I would never hurt myself,

Especially not over them.

People say they care,

If you have that, hold onto it,

And love them back.

Love them with every fiber of your being.

The ones I've known,

The ones I've had,

Have taken the knife.

They've taken that knife and stabbed.

Et tu?

These are the bleeding years.

These are the bleeding years.

Your Creation

Here I wake on a stainless bed,

Not even a pillow for my head.

I feel no pain, nothing at all.

Can't speak, can't scream, can't call.

You stand there like an angel of light,

Dressed in surgical white.

Hair pulled up, smile on your lips,

With scalpels, tongs, forceps, clips.

Can you move your hands?

Can you move your toes?

The two of us,

No one else knows.

Your creation,

My devastation.

Look what you've done to me.

Your creation,

Re-animation.

What have you done to me?

I don't remember what was said

I just remember being dead.

A car crash, I think there was a tree,

And that was the end of me.

You found me, brought me to your lab,

Laid me on this metal slab,

Made connections, stitches, splints.

My skin still has a grayish tint.

Can you move your hands?

Can you move your toes?

The two of us,

No one else knows.

Your creation,

My devastation.

Look what you've done to me.

Your creation,

Re-animation.

What have you done to me?

Do you think that I'll love you?

Think I'm your slave?

Give me orders,

I have to obey.

You brought me back.

You made me new.

The most hideous beast

You ever knew.

Your creation,

My devastation.

Look what you've done to me.

Your creation,

Re-animation.

What have you done to me?

What have you done to me?

What the hell have you done to me?

Why didn't you just let me stay dead?

Litmus Test

Are you my friend?

Are you really my friend?

What can I do for you?

That's the real measure,

Isn't it?

Let's test this out,

The scientific method.

Put your finger right her.

Yes, right here on this paper.

Oops, red,

pH 1.

Acidic,

Caustic.

Nope,

You're not my friend.

How about you?

Let's test this hypothesis.

Oh, no,

Blue.

pH 12.

Alkaline,

Corrosive.

I guess you're not my friend, either.

Guess I should have known.

There's nothing else I can do for you right now.

You don't need me.

I should have known.

<u>Otherwise, the Pain</u>

Just awakened by the sound of chimes,

With a tired hand I brush the night's crust from my eyes.

I lay in bed,

Contemplating,

Calculating my next few moves,

Otherwise,

The pain.

I have coughed for a week,

And my stomach feels like I've performed a thousand sit-ups,

Which I clearly have not.

I push back the cover and slowly slide my legs off the bed.

I sit up,

But the pain is still there,

But not as bad as expected.

The room is warm,

Warmer than I like,

But it's the price to pay for winter comfort.

In the bathroom,

I relieve myself and wash my hands.

The mirror looks back at me,

Appraising.

I don't think it approves,

And I don't feel like caring.

I turn on the water,

Drop my clothes to the floor,

And step into the shower.

For at least a full two minutes,

I do nothing but allow the hot water to run over my hair,

Down my face,

Down my back.

It feels good on the sciatica.

I scrub away the oil and the dead skin,

Scrub, scrub, scrub,

Until my skin is pink.

My hair is in my face,

And I push it back behind my ears.

I turn off the water finally and turn around,

Shaking away the water droplets like a dog.

The shower glass walls are steamed.

I take my index finger and trace on a panel,

"I love you, Jesus + Mom + Dad,"

The I draw a heart,

A cross,

And an ichthus.

On another panel,

I write,

"Thank you."

I dry off as much as I can before I step out,

Then finish up on the cold tile floor.

My head aches.

My stomach aches.

My hands ache.

My knees ache.

My back aches.

I look at the time on my phone,

The I glance down at my clothes on the floor.

What the hell,

I think,

And I put yesterday's clothes back on.

I have sick time saved up.

I feel sick.

I climb back into bed.

I will otherwise tomorrow.

Today is just pain.

<u>Trade</u>

Can I trade the living for the dead?

It no longer matters what was done or said.

There is love, and there is hate,

And the days speed towards the date.

Tears.

Silence.

A broken coffee cup on the floor,

Muddy footprints leading out the door,

And I run,

Not to somewhere, not to someone.

I will not pick up those pieces.

I am tired of drawn-out speeches.

I'm tired of an aching mind.

Sometimes I wish I were deaf and blind,

But then I realize the problem is you,

And I wish there was a refund,

And I wish it was done.

I would trade you in an instant.

The living for the dead, my intent,

But I know if you choke,

Or if you have a stroke,

The end would be the same.

I have lost my name.

Bastard, you,

So dumb, so numb, I choose

To walk away and bit my lip

Before the words would slip.

Bastard, you,

I choose.

Tears.

Silence.

Listening.

I call to the grave to make a trade.

I call out to the grave to make that trade.

I can't have them, and I won't have you.

I choose.

ABOUT THE AUTHOR

Steve Cain is originally from Augusta, Georgia and now makes his home in New Richmond, Ohio with his wife, Theresa, his kids, Samantha and Ethan, three dogs, a cat, and a plethora of deer and turkeys. He is a Certified Safety Professional by day. His first book, *The Great Inevitable,* was published in 2019 through Losantiville Press. His other books are available on Amazon or through the author. He is also the lead singer for the Christian metal band, Wars and Rumors. You can connect with Steve on Facebook (Steve Cain Writer), on Twitter (@stevecainwriter), and on Instagram (19stevecain72). If you enjoy his writing, please leave a review on Amazon and Goodreads. Thank you!

www.ingramcontent.com/pod-product-compliance
Lightning Source LLC
Chambersburg PA
CBHW060918140726
47996CB00001B/300